Long ago in a land called Phrygia,
there lived a king called Midas.

He was rich and kind,
but sometimes very foolish.

He lived in a splendid palace with his daughter, Zoe. He loved her dearly, even more than his famous rose garden.

By Julia Jarman

Illustrated by Claudia Venturini

First published in 2009 by
Franklin Watts
338 Euston Road
London
NW1 3BH

Franklin Watts Australia
Level 17/207 Kent Street
Sydney
NSW 2000

Text © Julia Jarman 2009
Illustrations © Claudia Venturini 2009

The right of Julia Jarman to be identified as the author
and Claudia Venturini as illustrator of this Work has been asserted
in accordance with the Copyright, Designs and Patents Act, 1988.

A CIP catalogue record for this book is available
from the British Library.

ISBN 978 0 7496 8585 0 (hbk)
ISBN 978 0 7496 8589 8 (pbk)

Series Editor: Melanie Palmer
Series Advisor: Dr Barrie Wade
Series Designer: Peter Scoulding

Printed in China

Franklin Watts is a division of
Hachette Children's Books,
an Hachette UK company
www.hachette.co.uk

Every morning they walked in the garden, stopping to admire the lovely roses and breathe in their delicious scent.

One morning they found a strange
creature, half-man and half-goat,
sleeping under one of the bushes.

"What is *that*?" Zoe asked.

Her father smiled,

"It is the old satyr, Silenus."

"You drank too much wine last night, Silenus," said the king. The satyr woke up, groaning.

As they helped him to his feet, Midas told Zoe that Silenus was a friend of Dionysus, god of wine. Then suddenly ...

... there was a flash of lightning and a cloud of smoke!

And out of the smoke appeared
the god himself, Dionysus.

"Midas, thank you for looking after my old friend," he boomed. "Wish for anything you like and I will grant it. That is my reward to you."

"Anything?" said Midas.

"Yes, anything," said the god.

"I wish for everything I touch to turn to gold," said Midas, quickly. "Are you sure?" boomed Dionysus. "Think about it first."

But Midas didn't want to think.
He just wanted to be the richest
man in the world.

So the god granted his wish –
and the king's troubles began.

At first, King Midas was delighted.
He touched a table ...

and it turned to gold.

He touched one of his
lovely roses ...

and they all turned to gold.

"This is wonderful!" Midas cried. When he put his hand in the fountain, the water turned to gold.

Joyfully, he went to dinner and tried to eat, but the food turned to gold.

He tried to drink, but the wine
turned to gold.

"Father, what have you done?"
cried Zoe, putting her arms
around him and ...

she turned to gold!

Now shame and sadness
filled the king's heart.
"Dionysus, please undo the
wish," he begged.

But the god just said,
"Go to the river and cover
yourself with water."

25

King Midas thought about it.
What if *he* turned to gold? But
then he thought about Zoe. Life
without her was not worth living.

He rushed to the river, clutching her golden body, and plunged into the water!

He didn't turn to gold. Nor did the water. Best of all, his beloved daughter came back to life. His golden touch had gone!

But even now, people say that the water in that faraway river has a golden gleam.

Puzzle 1

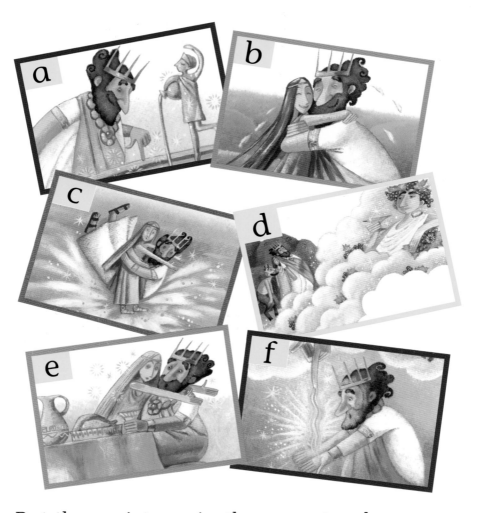

Put these pictures in the correct order.

Which event do you think is most important?

Now try writing the story in your own words!

Puzzle 2

Choose the correct speech bubbles for each character. Can you think of any others?

Turn over to find the answers.

Answers

Puzzle 1

The correct order is

1d, 2f, 3a, 4e, 5c, 6b

Puzzle 2

King Midas: 3, 4

Zoe: 1, 6

Dionysus: 2, 5

For more Hopscotch books go to: www.franklinwatts.co.uk

* hardback

Long ago, a poor woodcutter went to cut down an oak tree.

As he raised his axe,
a fairy appeared.
"Please leave this tree
alone," she begged.

4

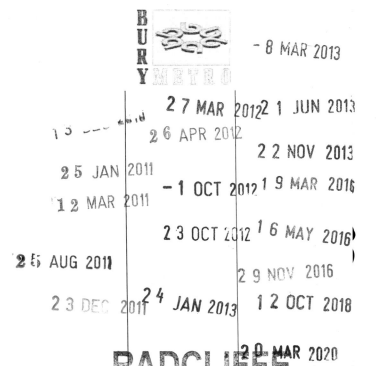

Illustrated by Stephen Holmes

First published in 2009 by
Franklin Watts
338 Euston Road
London
NW1 3BH

Franklin Watts Australia
Level 17/207 Kent Street
Sydney
NSW 2000

A CIP catalogue record for this book is available
from the British Library.

ISBN 978 0 7496 8608 6 (hbk)
ISBN 978 0 7496 8614 7 (pbk)

Series Editor: Jackie Hamley
Series Advisor: Dr Barrie Wade
Series Designer: Peter Scoulding

Printed in China

Franklin Watts is a division of
Hachette Children's Books,
an Hachette UK company.
www.hachette.co.uk

"Very well," replied
the woodcutter.

"Thank you," said the
fairy. "For your kindness,
I grant you three wishes.
Use them carefully!"

7

The woodcutter rushed
home to his wife.

"There is no food for supper," his wife said sadly.

"Never mind," laughed the woodcutter. "We need never be hungry again!"

He told his wife about
the three wishes.

"We could be rich," said
the woodcutter.

"Or famous," smiled his wife.

"Yes," said the woodcutter. "This thinking makes me hungry. I wish I could have a string of sausages."

A string of fat sausages appeared.

"You silly man!" cried
his wife. "You've wasted
a wish!"

16

"Oh no," cried the
woodcutter.

The wife kept moaning until the woodcutter got really cross.

"I wish these sausages were on the end of your nose!" he shouted.

The sausages flew up and stuck to his wife's nose.

"What have you done?"
she cried.

The wife pulled, but the sausages did not move.

The woodcutter pulled, but
the sausages were stuck.

"They don't look too
bad," said the woodcutter.

But his wife was so upset that the woodcutter felt sorry for her.

"I wish those sausages
would leave my wife's
nose," said the woodcutter
sadly, knowing this was
his last wish.

The string of sausages fell on to the table.

"Well, at least we're happy!" said the woodcutter.

"And we've got some nice sausages for supper!" laughed his wife.

Puzzle 1

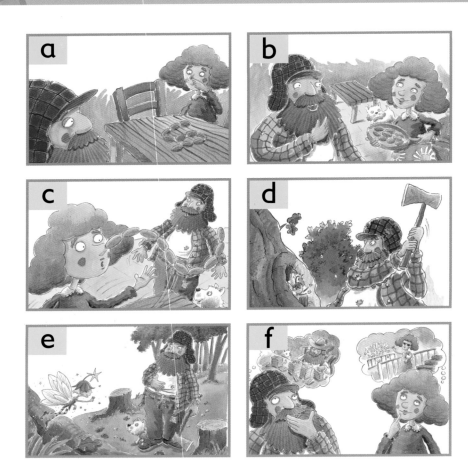

Put these pictures in the correct order.
Now tell the story in your own words.
What different endings can you think of?

Puzzle 2

generous   polite
bad-tempered

careful   careless
nasty

famous   cross
rich

Choose the correct adjectives for each character. Which adjectives are incorrect? Turn over to find the answers.

Answers

Puzzle 1

The correct order is: 1d, 2e, 3f, 4c, 5a, 6b

Puzzle 2

Fairy: the correct adjectives are generous, polite

The incorrect adjective is bad-tempered

Woodcutter: the correct adjective is careless

The incorrect adjectives are careful, nasty

Woodcutter's wife: the correct adjective is cross

The incorrect adjectives are famous, rich

Look out for Leapfrog fairy tales:

For more Leapfrog books go to: www.franklinwatts.co.uk